S0-AGH-997

06/2015

PALM BEACH COUNTY
LIBRARY SYSTEM
3650 Summit Boulevard
West Palm Beach. FL 33406-4198

THERE WAS AN OLD LADY WHO SWALLOWED A CHICK!

by Lucille Colandro
Illustrated by Jared Lee

Cartwheel
·B·O·O·K·S·®

SCHOLASTIC INC.
New York Toronto London Auckland
Sydney Mexico City New Delhi Hong Kong

With love for Philip and Sarah,
and with special thanks to the lunch bunch.
— L.C.

To Aunt Glennis,
a cool chick in her days
— J.L.

No part of this publication may be reproduced, stored in a retrieval system, or transmitted in any form or by any means, electronic, mechanical, photocopying, recording, or otherwise, without written permission of the publisher. For information regarding permission, write to Scholastic Inc., Attention: Permissions Department, 557 Broadway, New York, NY 10012.

ISBN: 978-0-545-16181-7

Text copyright © 2009 by Lucille Colandro.
Illustrations copyright © 2009 by Jared D. Lee Studios.

All rights reserved. Published by Scholastic Inc. SCHOLASTIC, CARTWHEEL, and associated logos are trademarks and/or registered trademarks of Scholastic Inc.

21 20 19 18 17   15/0

Printed in the U.S.A.   40
This edition first printing, January 2010

There was an old lady who swallowed a chick.
I don't know why she swallowed that chick,
but she didn't get sick.

There was an old lady who swallowed some straw.

The chick looked in awe as she swallowed the straw.
She swallowed the straw to cover the chick.
I don't know why she swallowed that chick,
but she didn't get sick.

There was an old lady who swallowed an egg.
She didn't beg to swallow that egg.

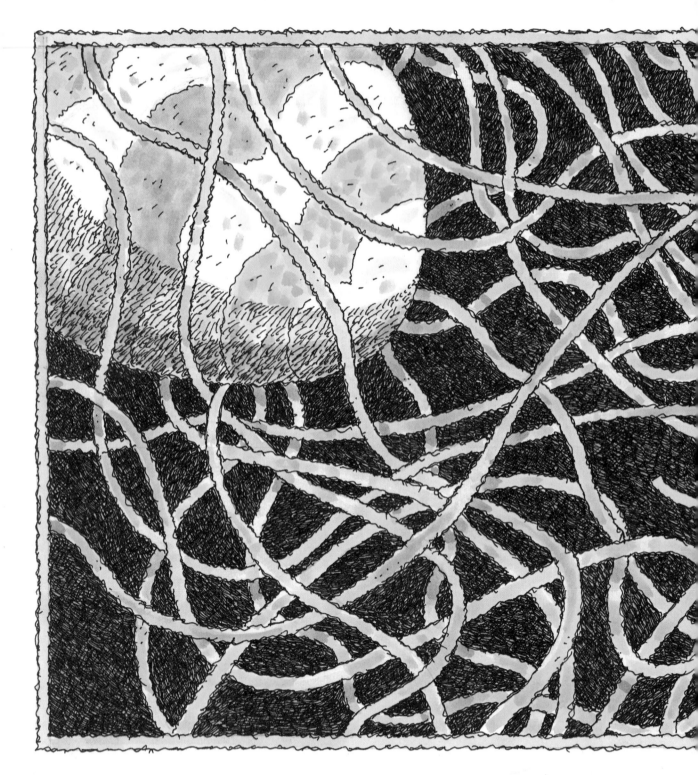

She swallowed the egg to jazz up the straw.
She swallowed the straw to cover the chick.

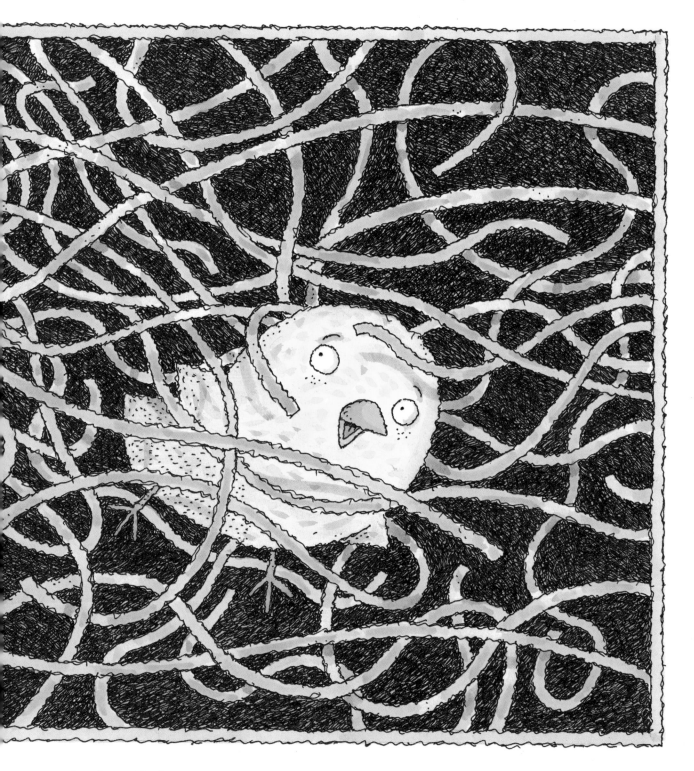

I don't know why she swallowed that chick,
but she didn't get sick.

There was an old lady who swallowed some candy.

She knew the candy would come in handy.

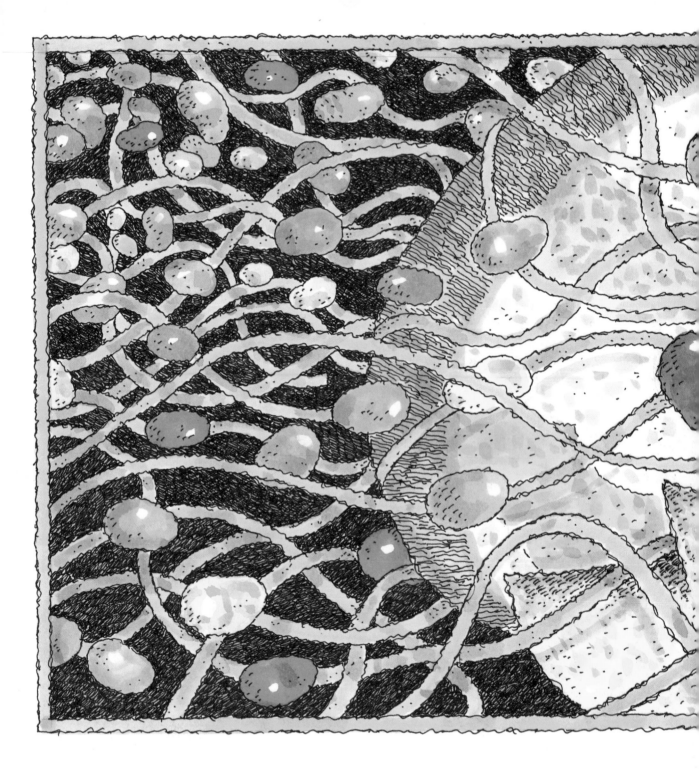

She swallowed the candy to sweeten the egg.
She swallowed the egg to jazz up the straw.

She swallowed the straw to cover the chick.
I don't know why she swallowed that chick,
but she didn't get sick.

There was an old lady who swallowed a basket.

A tisket, a tasket, a brightly colored basket.

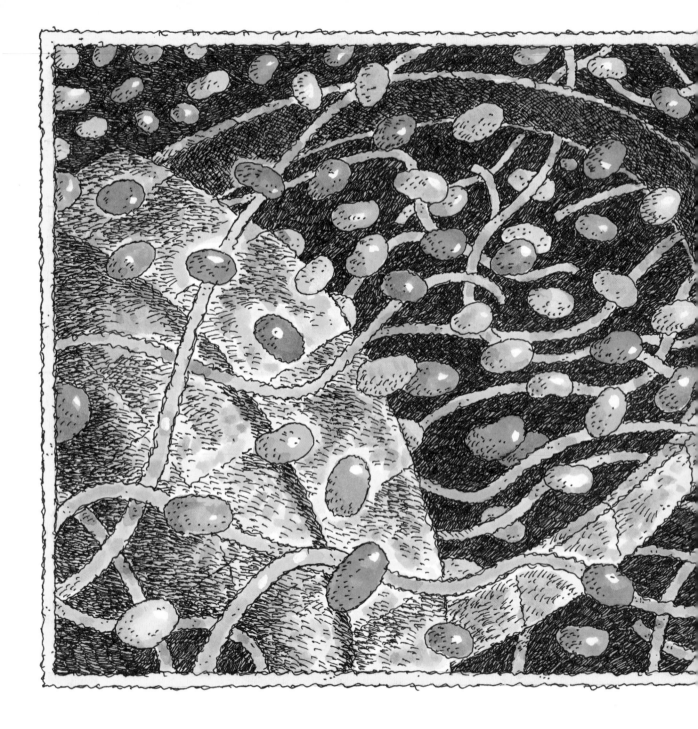

She swallowed the basket to carry the candy.
She swallowed the candy to sweeten the egg.

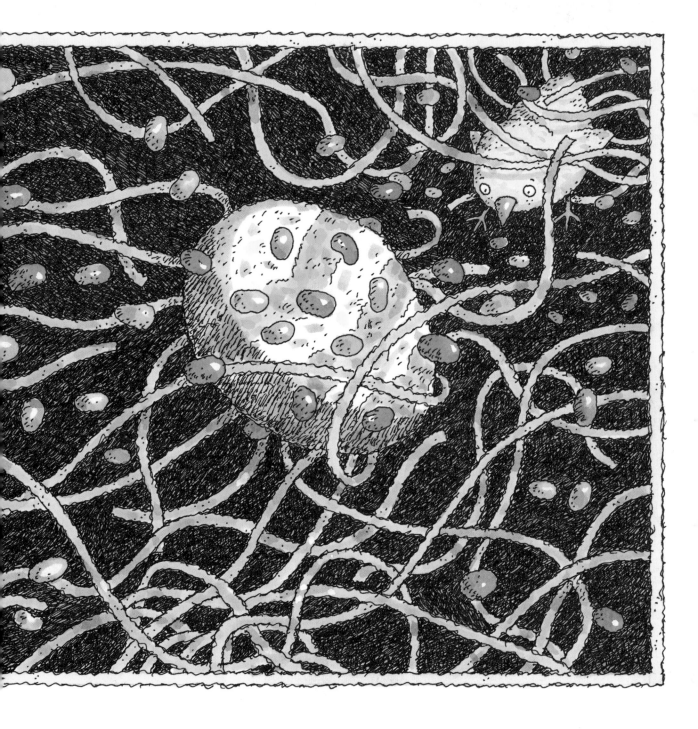

She swallowed the egg to jazz up the straw.
She swallowed the straw to cover the chick.
I don't know why she swallowed that chick,
but she didn't get sick.

There was an old lady who swallowed a bow.

Oh, what a show, when she swallowed that bow.

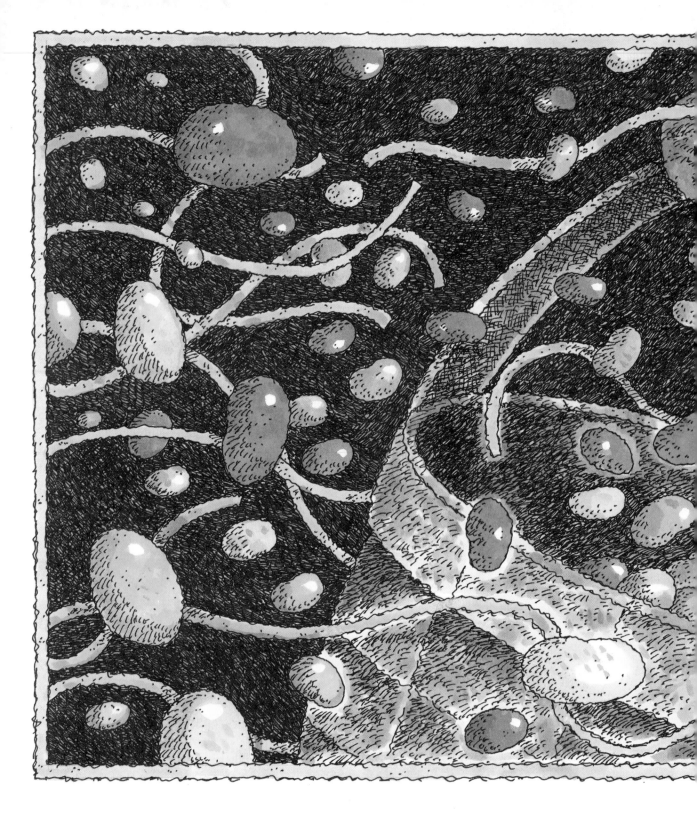

She swallowed the bow to tie on the basket.

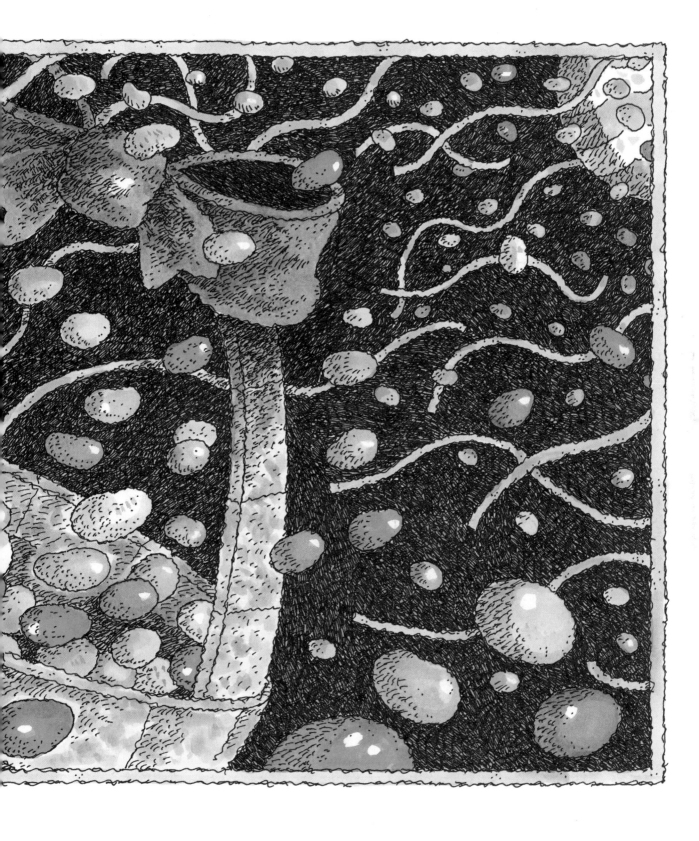

She swallowed the basket to carry the candy.

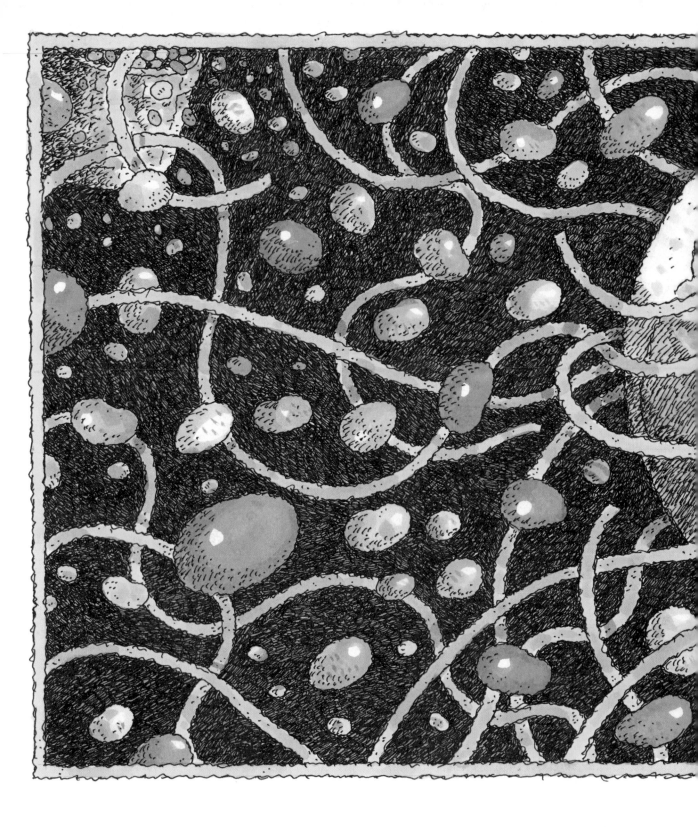

She swallowed the candy to sweeten the egg.

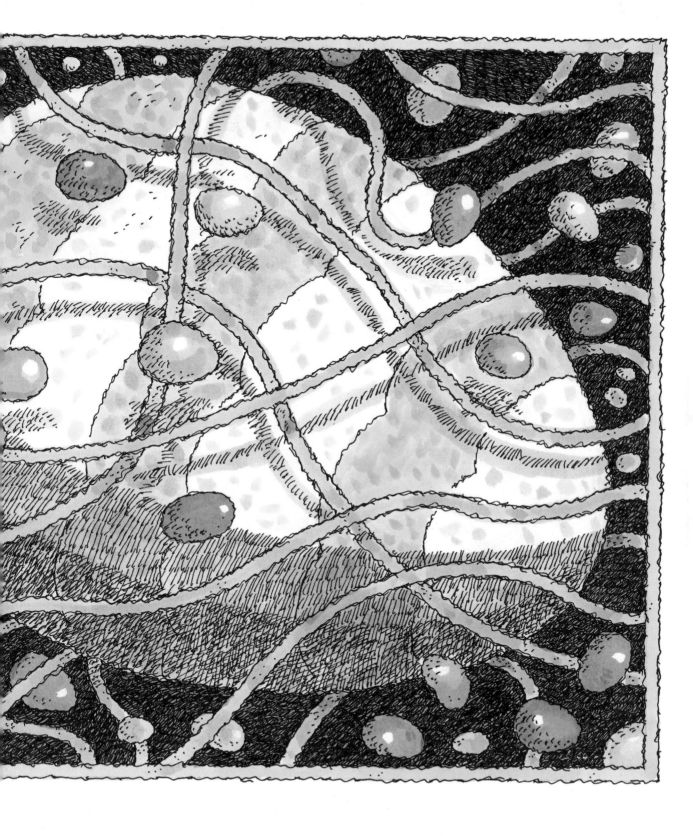

She swallowed the egg to jazz up the straw.

She swallowed the straw to cover the chick.

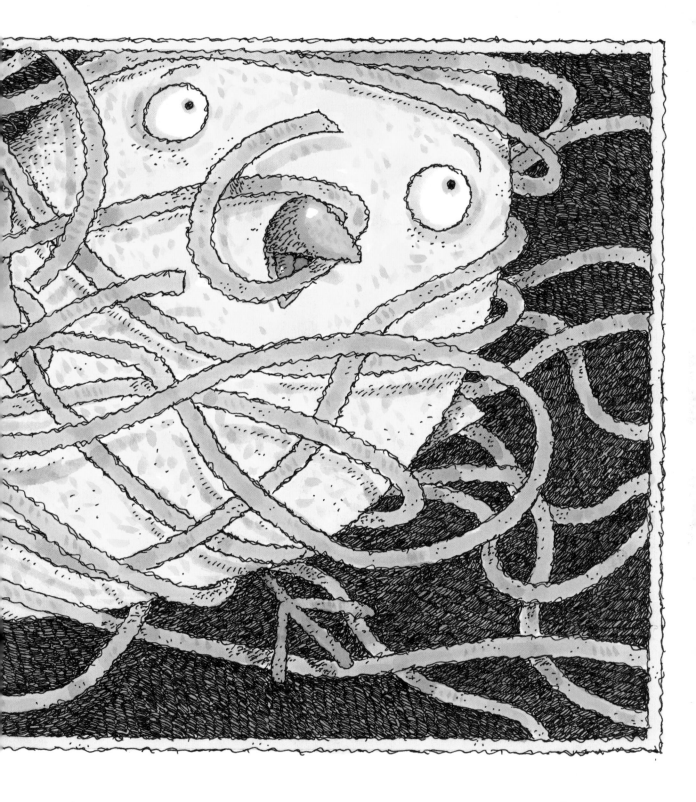

I don't know why she swallowed that chick,
but she didn't get sick.

There was an old lady who started to hop.

She jumped up and down and just wouldn't stop.

As she skipped down the trail
on a day that was sunny,

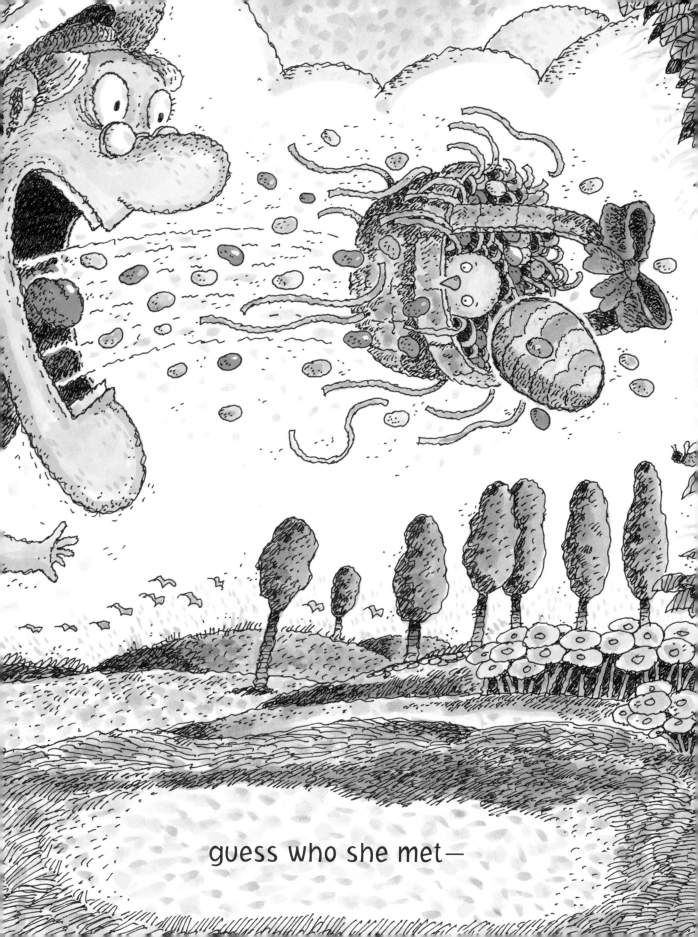

guess who she met—

Happy Easter!